P9-CRD-942

Baya, Baya, Lulla-by-a

For Suzanne ~ M. M.
For Venki ~ V. R.

✿

Atheneum Books for Young Readers
An imprint of Simon & Schuster Children's Publishing Division
1230 Avenue of the Americas
New York, New York 10020

Book design by Sonia Chaghatzbanian
The text of this book is set in Garamond.
The illustrations are rendered in watercolor.
Manufactured in China
First Edition

2 4 6 8 10 9 7 5 3 1

Library of Congress Cataloging-in-Publication Data
McDonald, Megan.
Baya, baya, lulla-by-a / Megan McDonald ; illustrated by Vera Rosenberry.
p. cm.
"A Richard Jackson book."
Summary: As a mother in rural India sings to her baby,
a weaverbird builds a nest for its young.
ISBN 0-689-84932-X
[1. Mother and child—Fiction 2. Weaverbirds—Fiction.
3. Lullabies—Fiction. 4. India—Fiction.] I. Rosenberry, Vera, ill. II. Title.
PZ7.M1487 Bay 2003
[E]—dc21 2001053611

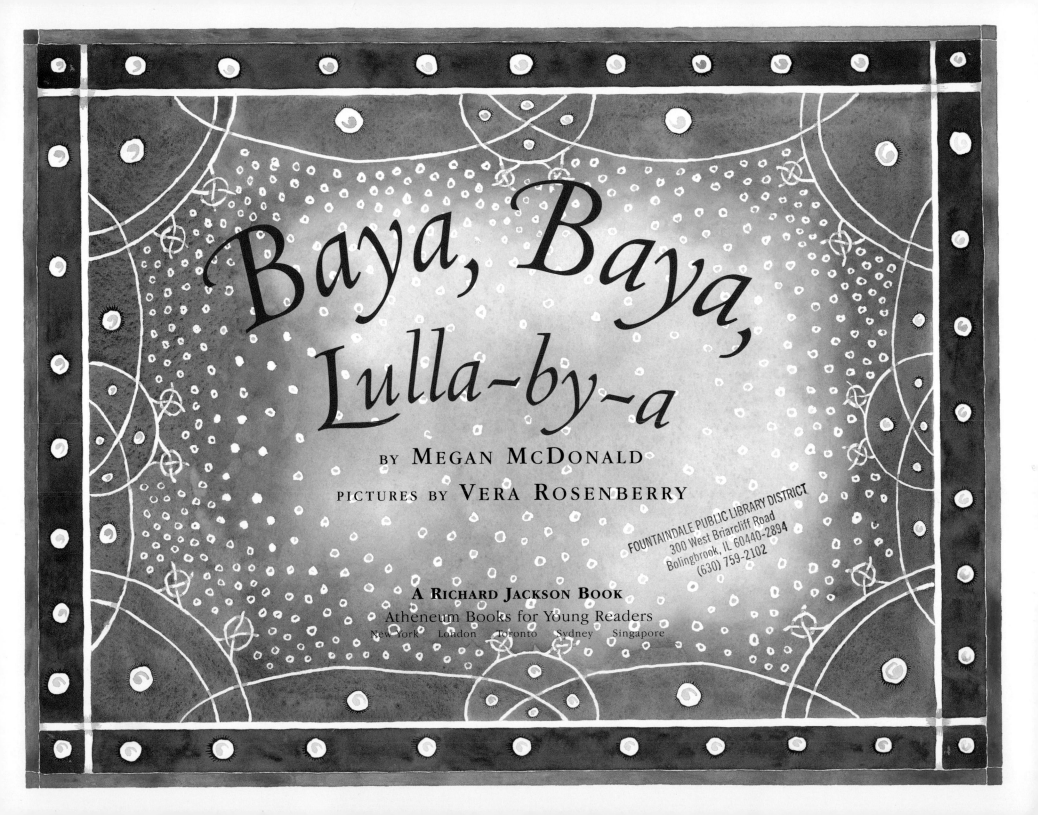

Baya, Baya, Lulla-by-a

BY MEGAN MCDONALD

PICTURES BY VERA ROSENBERRY

A RICHARD JACKSON BOOK
Atheneum Books for Young Readers
New York   London   Toronto   Sydney   Singapore

When the Wise Man whispers
pani, pani,

the river smells of new mud,

swells with monsoon rain, rain.

Chiri-ya! Chiri-ya!

sings the sun-yellow baya bird

from the old thorn tree.

Baya, baya, lulla-by-a.

Mata rocks you, *choti ladki,*

to the east, to the west,

to the land, to the sea.

You blink to the jingle, jingle of Mata's silver.

She sings to you morning after morning,

like a sleepy cricket.

Kira, kira.

Your heart answers, a small drum.

Dholak, dholak.

Baya Bird flits, flutters, flies

among leafy shadows,

chiri-ya! chiri-ya!

collects green grasses, weaves a nest

swishhh swishhh,

strand

by strand

by willowy strand.

Mata listens by the shutter.

She eyes the bright-colored spools—

river green, sun red, sky blue,

saffron for sand, indigo for night—

all the colors of your safekeeping blanket.

Mata weaves,

wishhh wishhh,

thread

by thread

by whispering thread.

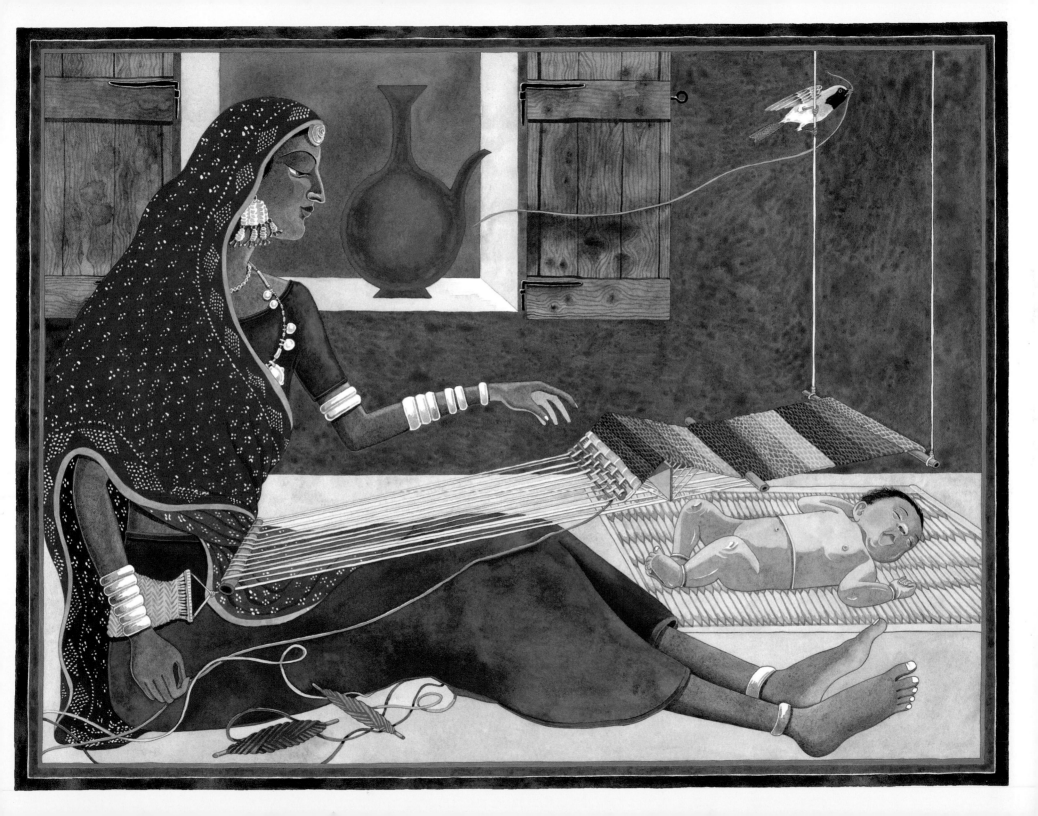

Baya Bird winds yellow flowers

in out over under

up down around

its vining, twining nest—

acacia petals laced

in a golden crown.

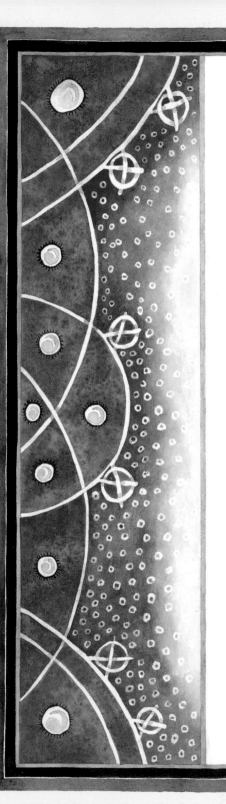

Mata ties and dyes the keeping cloth

in a pattern of stars.

She embroiders tiny mirrors,

wink, blink, wink, blink,

into a shimmering sky.

Look! Mother, baby, mother, baby, mother, baby.

When the last thread is tied,

Mata wraps you in your first quilt,

the color of one hundred mornings,

like arms around you safe and warm,

your own snug nest.

Warm breezes sway the baya nest

high and away in the treetop.

Wind blows always at its back,

bhal, bhal.

Mata carries you to the well,

where the water ripples, ripples,

like so many golden crowns.

She knots her *chadr* branch to branch

in the thorn tree.

She cradles you in the scarf,

light as a weed,

swings you in your tiny hammock,

jhula, jhula.

Ree! Ree!
Ree! Ree!

Baya Bird calls a warning,

mother to mother.

Cobra curls in crook of tree

naga, naga,

snakes its way

along leafy limb,

slither slither slide, slither slither slide.

Mata swoops you up,

holds you tight,

rocks you in her arms.

Rock~a~bye, hush~a~bye,

choti ladki, little one.

She carries you home,

heartbeat to heartbeat,

through the pale green

haze of desert.

Mata will bathe you with a cup of water.

Lullay, my babe.

When that cup is empty,

Mata will feed you ripe, sweet mangoes.

Lullay, my child.

When those mangoes are no longer sweet,

Mata will weave you a garland of flowers.

Lullay, my girl.

When that garland of flowers fades,

Mata will pull down the moon for you.

Lullay, my bird.

When night falls with a hush

through a fine layer of dust,

Baya Bird dabs bits of clay,

here, there, here, there,

catches fireflies one by one by one,

adorns its nest

with a thousand tiny sparks—

a flickering lamp,

treeful of stars.

Long after the fireflies

go dark,

and the tree mouse has come

and gone,

and the mason wasp

is done,

and the spider's web

is spun,

Mata lifts the baya's nest

from the old thorn tree.

She hangs it in your doorway,

lights the lamp until it glows like opals,

a night-light to chase away the dark.

Fortune smiles on you

as the river sings itself

to sleep.

Lalo~loli, lalo~loli.

Baya, baya, lulla~by~a.

Hush, my one,

heart like a drum.

Sleep, my bird,

under your own

small moon.

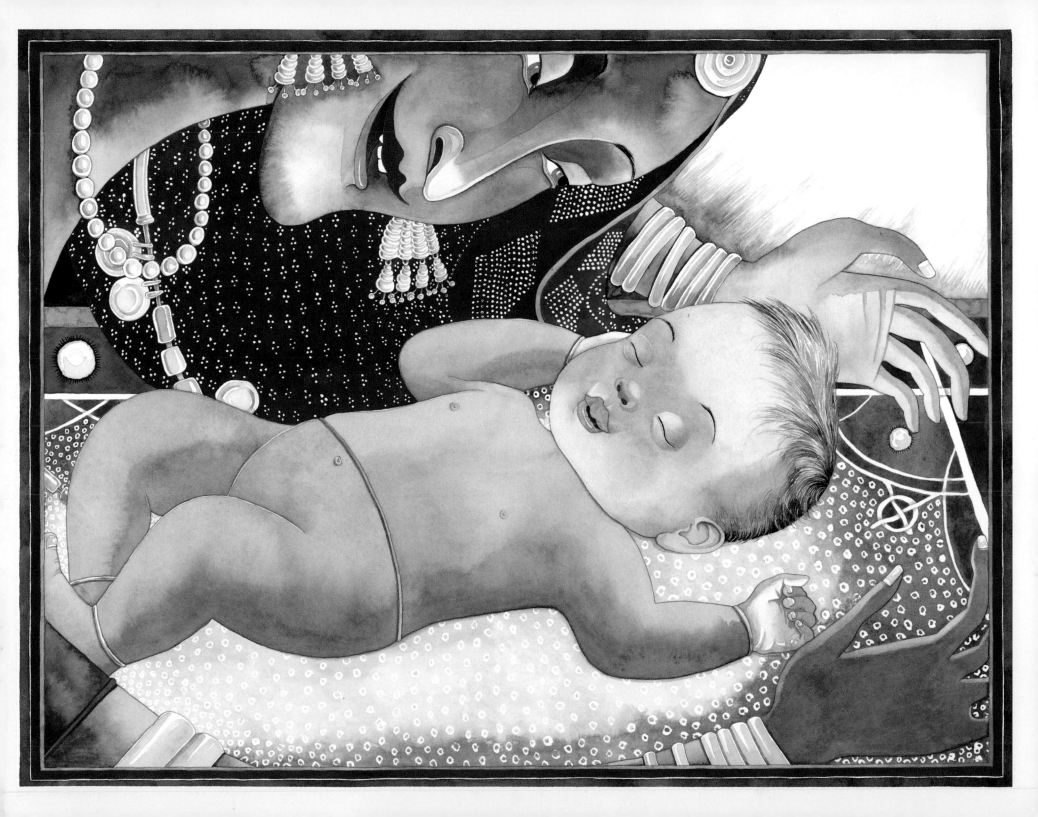

Hindi words:

❦

pani—water

chiriya—bird

Mata—mother

choti ladki—little girl

kira—insect

dholak—small drum

chadr—scarf

jhula—swing

bhal—wind

naga—cobra

During the monsoon, the baya bird of India weaves an intricate nest of grasses and decorates it with yellow flowers. In rural India, some say this weaver bird lights its nest in the night by dabbing it with clay and pressing fireflies to the clay, where they glow in the dark. When the baya bird leaves its nest, many creatures—including the tree mouse, the mason wasp, the spider—use it for shelter through the winter.

The empty nests also have many uses to the people of India—to strain sugarcane juice or buttermilk; as scrubbers; or as fuel. In tribal and rural areas, half-built nests are worn as caps by children or during local festivals, or carried as baskets to collect ripe fruit. Abandoned nests of these unusual weaver birds are also made into festive night lamps, decorated with strips of paper and bright bits of cloth, then hung in doorways for good fortune.

The lullaby that Mata sings is my own, inspired by the Indian lullaby, "Lalo Loli," by Ratan Devi and Ananda K. Coomaraswamy.